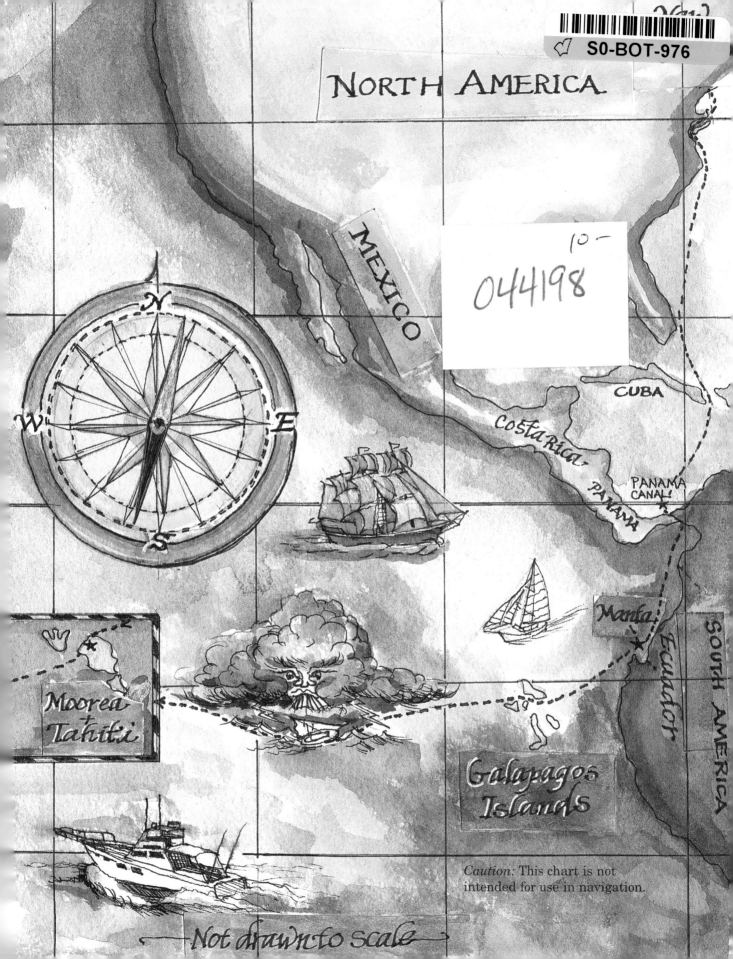

NORTH AMERICA

MEXICO

10-
044198

CUBA

Costa Rica

PANAMA

PANAMA CANAL!

Manta

Ecuador

SOUTH AMERICA

Moorea + Tahiti

Galapagos Islands

Caution: This chart is not intended for use in navigation.

Not drawn to scale

ISBN: 1-931807-26-4

Library of Congress Catalog Control Number: 2004110320

For information contact:
Bungee
c/o Ford
433 Bay Road
Durham, NH 03824

e-mail: sally@bravebungee.com
Toll free: 1-888-250-4862 voice & fax
Phone: 603-868-5850 voice & fax

Design: Grace Peirce

PETER E. RANDALL PUBLISHER LLC
P.O. Box 4726
Portsmouth, NH 03802
www.perpublisher.com

BUNGEE DOWN UNDER

by Sally Ford

illustrated by Peter Dudley

PETER E. RANDALL PUBLISHER LLC
Portsmouth, New Hampshire
2004

to my granddaughters

Anna Joan Laird
Helen Serena Laird

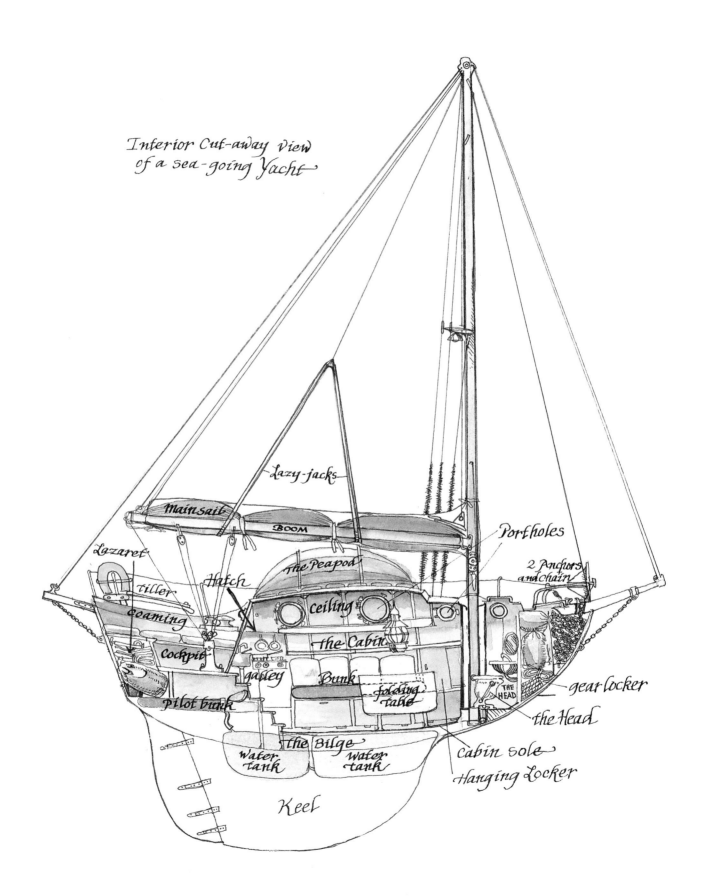

Interior Cut-away view
of a sea-going Yacht

Lazy-jacks

Mainsail

BOOM

Portholes

Lazaret

The Peapod

2 Anchors
and chain

Hatch

Tiller

ceiling

coaming

the Cabin

Cockpit

galley

Bunk

gear locker

THE
HEAD

Pilot bunk

folding
table

the Head

the Bilge

Cabin sole

water
tank

water
tank

Hanging Locker

Keel

Gypsy Rover danced in the dark upon the sea. Bungee sat below writing by the golden light of the lantern. Carefully her paw moved across the page. This is what Bungee wrote in the log:

Charlie's Charts says there is a coral reef ahead with a lagoon and a village called Mopelia. Plan to stop there for fresh fruit.

Bungee sailed all night. In the morning she could just make out the reef, a speck in the vastness of the sea.

As she sailed closer Bungee could see a glimmering line of waves breaking against the reef. She read Charlie's Charts again:

> Agitated water indicates the narrow entrance to the lagoon. It is one of the trickiest passes in the South Pacific.

"The water is not half as agitated as I am," muttered Bungee. The beautiful reef, hard as a rock, would tear *Gypsy Rover* to pieces if she hit it.

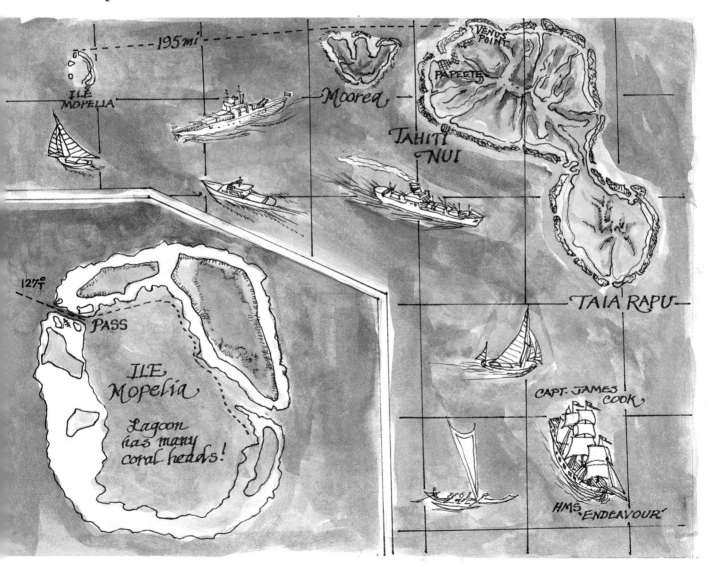

Looking through her binoculars, Bungee searched for the opening. There it was! A ribbon of deep green water streaming through the reef. The shallow water on either side was pale white.

The reef itself was dazzling shades of pink, made by billions and billions of tiny coral creatures piling atop each other, for thousand and thousands of years.

With the sun behind her, Bungee threaded her way through the narrow pass into Mopelia. Once safely inside, Bungee anchored *Gypsy Rover* in the lagoon, surrounded by a necklace of coral. The sound of the sea pounding against the reef became a lullaby. A thousand seabirds sang.

The entire village rushed out to welcome Bungee. "Come for a barbeque at the pink house on stilts," they said. Bungee rowed *Peapod* ashore, delighted to join them.

Eight grownups and two children lived on Mopelia. Their only contact with the outside world was by radio and a boat that came once a month to pick up the copra they made from dried coconuts.

Everyone sat on the beach feasting on roasted fish. "*Gypsy Rover* and I have sailed half way around the world to your enchanted island," Bungee told the villagers. "This is a dream come true."

A young man named Hiti asked Bungee to go lobstering. Bungee grabbed her mask and snorkel and jumped into his wooden dinghy. They motored out the narrow pass and along the reef as the sun set. Hiti gave a prayer for good hunting and safety from the sharks.

Bungee was small but she had a strong dog paddle. Even so it was a bit scary. There was no moon and Bungee swam through almost complete blackness. Hiti tugged at her paw. He flashed a light at a grinning shark.

Bungee bit down harder on her snorkel, but kept swimming, searching the bottom for lobsters. Then Hiti spotted one. Down Bungee dove, grabbed the lobster, and holding it high above her head, swam to the surface.

"Get the lobster out of the water as fast as you can," Hiti hollered. "Otherwise, the sharks will come." Bungee dumped the lobster into the dinghy. On the way back through the pass, Hiti taught Bungee the names of the stars in Tahitian.

Bungee wanted to stay longer in Mopelia, but she had to reach Australia before hurricane season. Bungee hoisted the red sails and worked her way out of the lagoon. As always at the start of a passage, Bungee felt seasick. She threw up over the side, munched on gingersnaps, and felt better by lunch.

Gypsy Rover sailed on through the South Pacific, waltzing between wind and waves, sunshine and starlight. One morning Bungee saw three dolphins sticking close to *Gypsy*. They leapt out of the water, glistening in the sun.

"You're getting close to Australia," said one of the dolphins, poking his smiling face out of the water. "We're here to guide you into Sydney."

The three dolphins stayed with *Gypsy Rover*, laughing and playing all day. Bungee followed the dolphins through Sydney Heads and into the harbor.

"Goodbye, Bungee," said the dolphins as they turned back to the sea. "Have fun!"

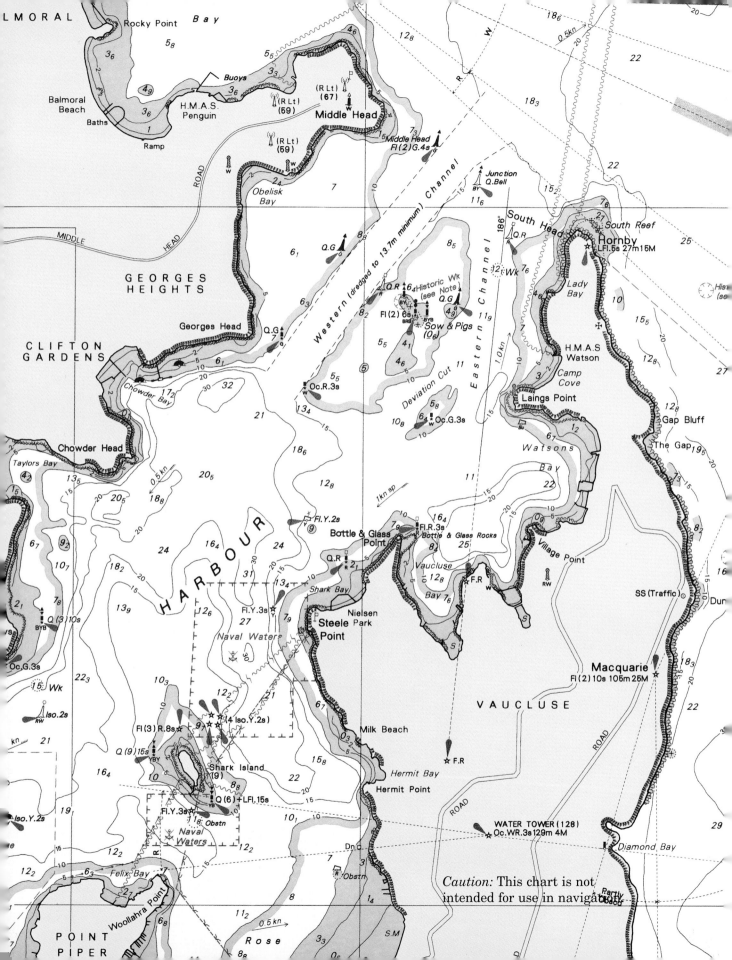

Caution: This chart is not intended for use in navigation.

Bungee found herself in one of the grandest harbors in the world. It was ringed with skyscrapers and filled with ferry boats, ocean liners, and sailboats darting about like hummingbirds. Bungee steered *Gypsy Rover* past the Sydney Opera House, reaching out like billowing white sails on Bennalong Point.

Circular Key was around the corner, and ahead, the great Sydney Harbour Bridge. Bungee sailed under the bridge and into a marina.

"G'day, mate," said a cheery voice as Bungee brought *Gypsy* smartly alongside the dock. "Toss me your line." The man made it fast to a cleat.

"Welcome to the land Down Under," said the man. "We're a big country. There's enough room here to swing a cat."

Bungee smiled sweetly. "I know I'm going to love Australia."

"Anything you need, you just ask. Captain Murray's the name. I'm the dock master. Don't get around as fast as I use to with this bad leg of mine, but anything you need, it's here. Water, showers, laundry. Ice. There's a grocery store down the road."

After an Australian breakfast of steak and eggs, Bungee began scrubbing *Gypsy* when she heard someone say "Hi. My name is Timmy." Bungee looked up.

This is what Bungee saw: a white motor yacht on the other side of the dock. A boy, who looked about six or seven, was waving to Bungee. A tall woman, dressed in white, stood beside the boy.

Bungee waved back. "Hi, I'm Bungee," she said. "Would you like to come aboard?"

"Please, Mother," said the boy. "May I go over and play?" The woman took the boy's hand. "No, no, Timmy! You can't play with that dirty little dog. And look at her boat. It is a mess. Now come along," said the woman.

"You'd look dirty too, lady, if you'd just sailed across the South Pacific," growled Bungee to herself.

"Come along, now, Timmy," said his mother. "I told you I do not want you to play with that dog. She's not our kind."

Squeezing out the sponge, Bungee dipped it in the soapy bucket again. "Don't worry, *Gypsy*," Bungee assured her, "I'll have you shipshape in no time."

Bungee spent all day scrubbing. When she finished Bungee took a long, hot shower. Bungee brushed her fur till it glistened.

"I'm going to *La Cenerentola*," Bungee told *Gypsy*. "That means Cinderella in Italian. Captain Murray will look after you while I am at the opera."

"No worries," said the Captain. "I'll take good care of her."

Bungee, looking very pretty in her party dress, jumped off

Gypsy and slipped on her sandals. She glanced up at the white yacht. Bungee could see the name—*Witch of the Wave*—painted on the life rings. "That's what my friend the *Starcrest* Skipper calls a floating Clorox bottle," Bungee said gleefully to herself. There was Timmy leaning over the rail, waving.

Bungee waved back.

Bungee trotted up the dock and walked to the Sydney Opera House. On the steps she met the Pickerings who were old friends of her parents.

"So glad you could join us, Bungee," said the Pickerings. "Now, we'll pick up our tickets and then go to the Mozart Café for a light supper before the opera."

The conductor walked to the podium, the audience applauded, the curtain went up, the orchestra began. Bungee tingled right down to the tip of her tail.

At intermission Bungee and the Pickerings went out on the balcony, Sydney Harbour lapping at their feet. The Southern Cross hung in the sky. The full moon looked down at them. They sipped champagne and nibbled on dark chocolates from a little box wrapped in gold foil.

When Cinderella found her prince, Bungee clapped and clapped. "Thank you for such a special evening," Bungee told the Pickerings.

Humming the music from the opera, Bungee puttered about *Gypsy Rover* all the next morning. In the afternoon she stretched out in the cockpit and began splicing a new anchor line.

Bungee could see Timmy standing on the bow of *Witch of the Wave,* holding a fishing pole. All of a sudden Timmy leaned too far over the rail.

Down, down, down Timmy fell into the dark water below.

Bungee jumped up and raced to the end of the dock. She banged her paw on a cleat but she never hesitated. She dove in and swam as fast as she could. Timmy's head was above the water, his arms thrashing wildly about. Then the small blond head went under.

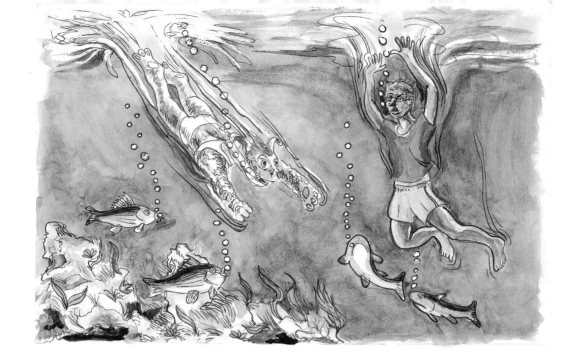

Bungee took a big breath, dove down, and put her paws around Timmy. She pulled him up to the surface.

"Hold on to me, Timmy," Bungee panted. "You're ok now. I've got you." Timmy, coughing and choking, clung to Bungee.

Keeping Timmy's head above water, Bungee swam back to the dock. Long arms reached down and pulled Timmy out.

Bungee was left to scramble out by herself.

"You tried to drown my son," cried Timmy's mother. "I knew all along you were a bad dog." She hugged Timmy closer to her. "You wicked dog. You bit my Timmy. He's bleeding."

Bungee tried to say, "No, no, the blood is from the cut on my paw," but no one listened.

"Bungee! Bungee! She was the one," sobbed Timmy.

"Yes, we know, son," said his father, his voice steely. "Hush now, we must get you out of these wet clothes. We'll talk about it tomorrow."

With one final "you wicked dog," off they swept.

Bungee limped back to *Gypsy Rover*. Wrapping a bandage around her paw, she crawled into her bunk.

Bungee lay there all alone.

She thought of her mother who would smooth her forehead and plump the pillows. Her daddy would hold her in his strong arms and say everything is going to be all right, Bungee.

Sad and sick, she slept fitfully, dreaming of home and the dark green firs along her river.

Bungee never heard Captain Murray knocking on the door of *Witch of the Wave* early the next morning. "Just came to look in on the boy," said the captain.

"Thank you," said Timmy's father. "We were so worried about him, but he's fine today."

"No thanks to that dreadful dog," Timmy's mother added.

"You've got it all wrong, ma'am," said Captain Murray. "I saw your boy fall overboard. I could never have gotten there fast enough, not with this gimpy leg of mine. It was Bungee who saved your son.

"But Bungee is one sick puppy," said Captain Murray. "Her paw's swollen up like a baseball. She needs a doctor and quick."

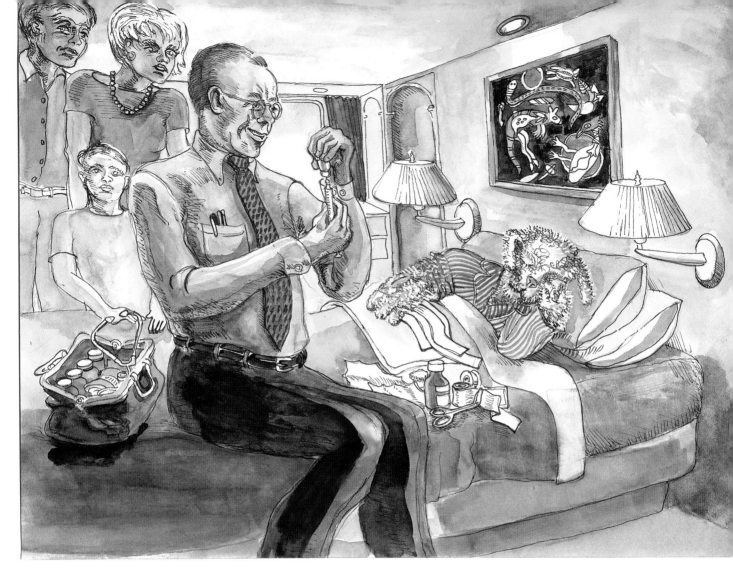

Moments later Bungee was gently carried aboard *Witch of the Wave*. "Put her in our stateroom where I can take care of her," said Timmy's mother.

"Yes, an infection," the doctor said as he examined Bungee. "That is a nasty cut. We've got to get the swelling down. You must give her a teaspoon of this antibiotic every four hours. I'll be back tomorrow to change her bandage."

All that day Timmy's mother sat beside Bungee, bathing Bungee's forehead with a cool washcloth and feeding her spoonfuls of chicken soup.

Timmy sat as close to Bungee as he could get. "Oh Bungee, please get better," he pleaded.

Timmy's father looked down at the little gray figure on the bed. "Oh Bungee, brave and true, if it hadn't been for you . . ." and his voice trailed off and he busied himself polishing his glasses.

Timmy's mother patted Bungee. "Oh, Bungee, I thought you were so different from us. I was wrong. Please forgive me."

All that day Bungee lay very still.

The next morning the doctor was smiling. "I was worried about that infection, but it looks like we've got it licked. Bungee can get up now as long as she doesn't overdo."

After that a familiar sight at the marina was a young blond boy with a gray dog at his side, skipping along together, chatting away. Bungee became like an older sister to Timmy. She taught him to swim. The two friends went to the zoo and held a koala bear and watched the kangaroos hopping about. Best of all, Bungee taught Timmy how to sail *Peapod.*

"Keep her footing, keep her footing, that's what the *Starcrest* Skipper always says," explained Bungee. "You can't just point the boat into the wind. You have to zigzag back and forth. If you want to come into the wind, you push the tiller away from you. If you pull the tiller towards you, the bow turns the other way."

One evening Captain Murray came to visit. He was carrying
five toy boats. "One for you, Timmy, and one for Bungee," said the
Captain.

"Made them myself out of plywood. See the pointy end is the
bow. The square end is the stern. And that's the sail," he said,
pointing to a birthday candle near the bow of each little boat.

Everyone walked down to the end of the dock. The sun was setting. The great harbor was still. They all knelt down.

Captain Murray lit a match and cupped his hand around the flame. Carefully he lit each candle. The candles flickered, then flowered into a golden flame. Leaning over the dock, they slipped the toy boats into the water.

"Now close your eyes and make a wish," said Captain Murray.

"I wish," said Timmy, "that Bungee could stay with us forever and ever."

"Yes, Bungee, you are part of our family now," said Timmy's mother.

"And I wish I could stay with you," Bungee said quietly. "But *Gypsy Rover* is waiting for me. I must follow my dream to sail around the world back to the dark green firs of home."

"We understand," said Timmy's father. "But you will always have a home with us wherever you are."

"Thank you," said Bungee, her nose beginning to tickle.

Captain Murray cleared his throat and said, "This might be the time for a bit of poetry about the gallant Ulysses who sailed the wine-dark sea in days of yore. You'll grow to love the poem as I do when you're older. It goes like this." He cleared his throat again and began:

> *Come, my friends*
> *'Tis not too late to seek a newer world.*
> *Push off, and sitting well in order smite*
> *The sounding furrows; for my purpose holds*
> *To sail beyond the sunset, and the baths*
> *Of all the western stars. . . .*

They all sat close together on the dock watching the tiny flotilla sail out upon Sydney Harbour. The little boats bobbed along bravely to the open sea, their candles burning brightly.

THE LANGUAGE OF THE SEA

Cabin – the living room (and usually the kitchen) of a boat. You "go below" from the cockpit to the cabin.

Galley – the kitchen.

Head – the bathroom.

Ceiling – unlike a house, the ceiling is the wall of the cabin.

Cabin sole – the floor of the cabin.

Bilge – under the cabin sole at the bottom of the boat where water collects. The bilge always needs pumping!

Hatch – the sliding top of the door leading down into the cabin.

Portholes – the windows in the cabin.

Bunks – the beds.

Hanging locker – the closet, usually very small, for hanging clothes and foul weather gear.

Lazaret – a space in the stern of the boat used for storage.

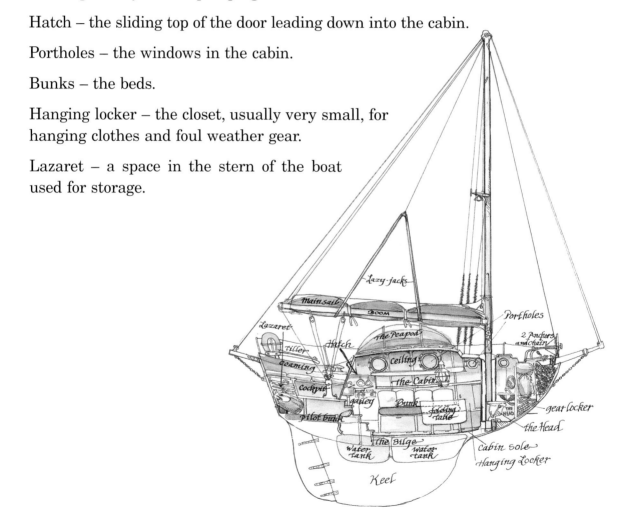

THE LANGUAGE OF THE SEA

Bow – the pointy end of the boat.

Stern – the other end.

Starboard – the right side of a boat as you face the bow.

Port – the left side of a boat as you face the bow. An easy way to remember: Left and Port both have four letters and end with T.

Mast – the tall pole growing out of the boat like the tall tree in the forest that it once was.

Sail – the sail goes up the mast and catches the wind. The jib is the smaller sail near the bow.

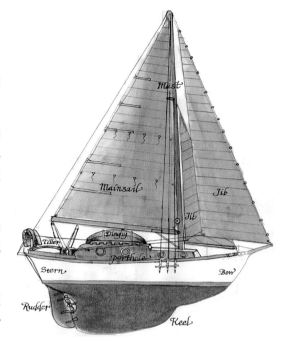

Tiller – the stick that is attached to the rudder that steers the boat. Some boats have a wheel instead of a tiller.

Deck – the deck is the roof of the boat. The cabin is what you step down into from the cockpit.

Sextant – an instrument for measuring the position of the boat by taking a "sight" against the stars or the sun and then doing calculations that show where you are. A sextant was always used before the modern day GPS, but a good sailor still knows how to use a sextant.

Dinghy – the little boat used to get to the big boat. The *Peapod* is Bungee's dinghy for *Gypsy Rover*.

ACKNOWLEDGMENTS

- When Bungee checks Charlie's Charts, she is reading from one of the excellent cruising guides written by the late Charles E. Wood and his wife Margo. I am grateful to Margo Wood for permission to paraphrase from *Charlie's Charts of Polynesia: the South Pacific, East of 165 W. Longitude.* The book includes anchorages, passage times, weather, and entry procedures for the different areas.

- A part of the chart of Sydney Harbour is printed actual size with the permission of the Australian Hydrographic Service of the Royal Australian Navy. The full chart, Port Jackson, AUS 200, is $46\frac{1}{2}$" wide and $28\frac{1}{2}$" high and shows even more of the vastness of Sydney Harbour. Charts such as this are used by sailors all over the world.

- When Bungee goes to the Sydney Opera House for *La Cenerentola* (pronounced *chen er en toll a*) she is seeing one of the loveliest operas in the world. Written by Gioacchino Rossini and based on the fairy tale of Cinderella, it was first performed in Rome in 1817.

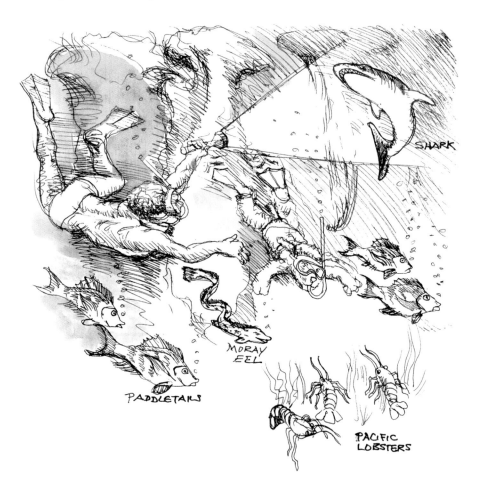

SHARK

MORAY EEL

PADDLETAILS

PACIFIC LOBSTERS

- The *Witch of the Wave* was a real ship. The name is taken from the magnificent three-masted clipper ship built in Portsmouth, New Hampshire in 1851 by George Raynes. She set a record, eighty-one days from Calcutta to Boston, which has never been beaten. The *Witch* ended her days in Norway renamed *Ruth*.
- I am grateful to Valerie England for the idea of the toy boats. As a Girl Scout Leader, Val and her young troops made the little boats, lit the candles, and set them afloat on summer evenings. Forty years later some of Val's Girl Scouts still remember singing softly as they watched the boats bobbing upon the water. The boats can also be cut out from biodegradable cardboard.
- Captain Murray is reciting from *Ulysses*, one of the most powerful poems in the English language. Written by Alfred, Lord Tennyson in 1842, the poem tells the tale of the Trojan War and the sailor who made his long voyage home. The final words of the poem are "to strive, to seek, to find, and not to yield."

Bungee's Mail

Bungee loves to get mail, and if she isn't off with *Gypsy Rover* on a long passage, Bungee will answer you very promptly.

You may write Bungee a letter addressed to:

Bungee
c/o Sally Ford
433 Bay Road
Durham, New Hampshire
03824
U.S.A.

You may write Bungee an e-mail to:

bungee@bravebungee.com

Visit Bungee's website at www.bravebungee.com

BUNGEE'S MAILBAG

- Thank you for writing *Bungee's Voyage*. I really liked it. —Daniel from California, a blind seven-year-old sailor on a 48-foot power boat.

- A book that could become a children's classic. It has adventure, wit, and charm and is told with a lovely humorous lilt. —Kay from New Hampshire.

- Thank you for taking your time to e-mail Maddy. She enjoyed hearing from you. We enjoyed reading your book together. We talked a lot about the ocean, sailing, and continents. —Maddy's Mommy, from Maine.

- I read the book about your voyage around the world. What happened in the second half of your voyage? You were a brave dog to go around the world in a sailboat. —Robert from Washington. (P.S. Robert received *Bungee's Voyage* as a gift from his grandparents. It was the first challenging book that he read aloud to me—and he kept at it because he so enjoyed the story! Thanks.—Robert's Mom)

- I would like to order 20 more copies of *Bungee's Voyage*. It contains so many wonderful principles and images that I find myself referring to Bungee again and again! At the end of the year I want to present each student with a copy to keep. —Diane, second-grade teacher from New York.

ABOUT THE AUTHOR

Sally Ford lives on Great Bay in Durham, New Hampshire, with her husband Dan and two Maine coon cats, Hermione and Harry Potter. Sally sails a little boat called *Gone With the Wind*.

ABOUT THE ILLUSTRATOR

Peter Dudley lives in Providence, Rhode Island, with his wife, fellow artist Margaret Skalski. Peter teaches at his alma mater, the Rhode Island School of Design, and at the Attleboro Museum Center for the Arts.